CAPTAIN FACT's

ROMAN ADVENTURE

THE WORLD'S FIRST NON-FICTION SUPERHERO

BY J & G PACKER

EGMONT

KNIFE & PACKER FACT!

KNIFE AND PACKER FACT!
IF KNIFE AND PACKER COULD GO BACK
TO ANCIENT ROME THEY'D LOVE TO BE
INVITED TO ONE OF THE EMPEROR'S
FABULOUS PARTIES. NOT ONLY WOULD
THE FOOD AND DRINK FLOW, BUT IT
WOULD BE A GREAT EXCUSE TO WEAR
A TOGA!

First published in Great Britain in 2005
by Egmont UK Limited, 239 Kensington High Street, London W8 6SA

Text and illustrations copyright © 2005 Knife and Packer
The moral rights of the authors have been asserted.

ISBN 1 4052 1771 5

1 3 5 7 9 10 8 6 4 2

A CIP catalogue record for this title is available
from the British Library

Printed and bound in Great Britain

CONTENTS

WITHDRAWN

STAR

CLIFF THORNHILL
TV'S WORST WEATHERMAN.

PUDDLES
THE ONLY
WEATHERDOG ON TV.

CAPTAIN FACT
THE WORLD'S FIRST
INFORMATION SUPERHERO.

KNOWLEDGE
CAPTAIN FACT'S
FAITHFUL SIDEKICK.

RING...

LUCY
HEAD OF MAKE-UP AND CLIFF'S BEST FRIEND.

THE BOSS
HE'S SCARY!

PROFESSOR MINISCULE
HEAD OF THE FACT CAVE AND THE BRAINS BEHIND MISSIONS.

FACTORELLA
PROFESSOR MINISCULE'S DAUGHTER AND ALL-ROUND WHIZZ-KID.

CHAPTER 1
THE HOLE STORY

TV'S WORST WEATHERMAN, Cliff Thornhill, and his sidekick, Puddles the dog, were at the airport . . .

'Our first holiday in years!' said Cliff excitedly. 'Now, did you pack everything, Puddles?'

'All the important things,' whispered Puddles, who kept his voice down in public. 'Passport, chilli-flavoured dog biscuits, swimming trunks, custard-flavoured dog biscuits, underwear, chocolate-flavoured dog biscuits, hair dryer, lemon-flavoured dog biscuits . . .'

HOT AIR

CHECK-IN

'I think you'll find they've got dog biscuits in Italy,' said Cliff, as they handed over their passports and tickets. 'I can't wait to visit Sir Ramsbottom Tickell's new museum.'

Cliff and Puddles were off to visit the world's most famous archaeologist, Sir Ramsbottom Tickell, who had recently opened a museum in Rome to house all the treasures he'd unearthed around the world.

Cliff handed over the passports. In no time he and Puddles were sitting in their seats awaiting take-off.

'Comfy seat, great!' said Puddles, settling in.

'Fantastic in-flight entertainment, Puddles,' said Cliff, beaming. 'There's a documentary on cloud formations!'

As the plane started to taxi down the runway before take-off, Cliff and Puddles noticed something strange.

'That's the weirdest looking plane I've ever seen,' said Puddles, 'it seems to be having some trouble getting off the ground.'

'That's not a plane,' said Cliff, 'that's THE BOSS!'

'THORNHILL! GET OFF AT ONCE!' screeched the Boss. 'ALL HOLIDAYS ARE CANCELLED!'

As the plane ground to a halt, all the other passengers were staring at Cliff and Puddles.

'This is *soooooo* embarrassing,' hissed Cliff as they trudged off the plane. Awaiting them on the tarmac was the Boss.

'I'd just got back from a month on the beach,' said the Boss, 'when news came through to the private jet. There's been a catastrophe at the Tickell Museum in Rome. Hop into the limousine, I'll explain on the way to the studio.'

In the car the Boss continued. 'The entire Museum is on the brink of collapsing into the ground. I want all the staff working on this story – even you, Thornhill.'

'Is Sir Ramsbottom inside?' asked Cliff.

'Not just him: he was giving a guided tour to a party of school children. They're all trapped inside. And not only that, but the site has become unstable – it could give way at any minute.'

'Give way at any minute?' asked Cliff uneasily. 'How can that be possible?'

'Turns out the Museum was built on an unstable Ancient Roman site!' said the Boss. 'Rescue teams can't go anywhere near it.'

As soon as they got to the studio, Cliff and Puddles bumped into Lucy, Cliff's friend from the Make-up Department.

'Hey, aren't you two meant to be on holiday?' said Lucy. 'Have you heard the news . . . ?'

'Can't stop, Lucy,' shouted Cliff as they burst into their office. He turned to Puddles. 'You know what's next, Puddles: **THIS IS A MISSION FOR CAPTAIN FACT!**'

FACT CAVE

'We've got to save that museum,' said Captain Fact, as they sped down the corridors of the Fact Cave on the new Fact Scooters. 'We need to know how much longer that Roman building will hold out, before it and the Tickell Museum collapse.'

'The Romans must have been pretty rubbish at building,' said Knowledge.

'Actually the Romans were very good at building,' said Captain Fact. 'Ker-Fact! The Colosseum, Rome's huge arena, could seat 50,000 people and yet everyone could leave in a couple of minutes!'

'I suppose that's fallen down too,' said Knowledge, trying not to sound impressed.

'No, it's still standing,' said Captain Fact. 'Just like many other Roman buildings that have survived for thousands of years.' And with that his teeth began to chatter . . .

FACT

FACT

BY MIXING LIME WITH VOLCANIC SOIL, THE ROMANS INVENTED CONCRETE IN THE 2ND CENTURY BC.

FACT

ROMAN ROADS WERE STRAIGHT SO THAT THE ARMY COULD GET AROUND THE ROMAN EMPIRE QUICKLY. THEY WERE SO WELL MADE THAT SOME OF THEM ARE STILL AROUND TODAY!

FACT

THE ROMANS WERE THE FIRST TO USE DOMES IN THEIR BUILDINGS. THE BIGGEST WAS IN THE PANTHEON - IT WAS THE BIGGEST DOME IN THE WORLD FOR OVER 2,000 YEARS.

'Wow!' said Knowledge, 'I'd love to see an ancient Roman kennel. It probably had an enormous dome, hot and cold running gravy and a road straight to the dog-biscuit factory.'

'You may well get the chance,' said Captain Fact ominously, hitting the brakes on his Fact Scooter. As they parked up outside the Nerve Centre, the door was already sliding open . . .

CHAPTER 2
THERE'S NO PLACE LIKE ROME

'*SALVE* CAPTAIN FACT and Knowledge!' said Professor Miniscule, the world's shortest genius and the brains behind the Fact Cave. 'There you are, at last!'

SALVE! GENTLEMEN

'*Salve?*' said Knowledge. 'Are you feeling all right, Professor Miniscule?'

'Professor Miniscule is fine,' said Captain Fact. '*Salve* is Latin for hello. Ker-Fact! The Ancient Romans spoke Latin. Many of our words today come from Latin: for example, our word 'false' is from the Latin *falsus*.'

'This is no time for a language lesson,' said Professor Miniscule tetchily, 'you've got an archaeologist to dig out of a hole ...

19

Now, you know the Tickell Museum is currently collapsing into the ground,' Professor Miniscule continued sternly. 'I've identified the site the Museum was built on – it was a Roman gladiator school. Something must have happened there to make it unstable, and we need you to find out what.'

'Hang on, let me guess,' interrupted Knowledge. 'The bricks were made out of cotton wool? No, no, the walls were made out of chocolate? I know, the foundations were made out of toffee?'

'This is no time for games, Knowledge,' said Captain Fact, as Professor Miniscule started turning purple.

'Thank you,' said Professor Miniscule. 'The only way to save the Museum and everybody in it is for you to go back to Roman times to identify the problem with the building and fix it.'

'Back in time,' gulped Captain Fact and Knowledge, not for the first time.

'Yes, back 2,000 years,' said Professor Miniscule, before pressing a button on his control panel. 'I give you the Time Portal.'

Before them materialised a gleaming virtual doorway.

'Yes, the Time Portal,' said Professor Miniscule. 'Step through this and your particles will be catapulted back in time and reconstituted in Ancient Rome.'

Just then Factorella bounced in, dressed from head to toe in heavy duty workman's clothes.

'Hi, guys,' said Factorella, chirpily, 'I can't wait to investigate an Ancient Roman building. When do we get catapulted?'

'How many times do I have to tell you? You're too young to go on missions,' said Professor Miniscule. 'Now, have you programmed Factotum, the fact cave supercomputer, to brief Captain Fact and Knowledge?'

A BRIEF HISTORY OF ANCIENT ROME.

753 BC: ALTHOUGH NO ONE KNOWS FOR SURE, LEGEND HAS IT THAT ROME WAS FOUNDED ON THIS DATE. IT'S A GOOD SPOT FOR A CITY BECAUSE IT'S CLOSE TO THE SEA AND PROTECTED BY THE ALPS IN THE NORTH.

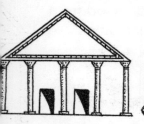

509 BC: WELL-ORGANISED TRADE AND DEFENSIVE SYSTEMS MEANT THAT ROME FLOURISHED, AND THE ROMAN REPUBLIC EXPANDED THROUGHOUT ITALY AND THE MEDITERRANEAN.

'Thanks, Factorella,' said Professor Miniscule. 'The Fact Scooters need recharging, now off you go!'

'But, Dad . . .' wheedled Factorella.

'But nothing,' said Professor Miniscule. 'And no speeding in the corridors like last time.'

As Factorella sidled off, Captain Fact and Knowledge stood nervously on the threshold of the Time Portal.

'The Time Portal has been set for Rome, AD 85,' said Professor Miniscule. 'Your time co-ordinates are spot on, but I can't guarantee you'll step out in the right place. The gladiator school is right next to the Colosseum, the biggest building in Rome – you should be able to spot it from miles off. Good luck, gentlemen.'

And Captain Fact and Knowledge stepped through the Time Portal.

SECRET FACT!

HOW DID THE FACT CAVE GET TO BE THE FACT CAVE?

THE FACT CAVE WASN'T ALWAYS THE TECHNO-BUSTING NERVE CENTRE THAT IT IS NOW . . .

CHAPTER 3

WHEN IN ROME...

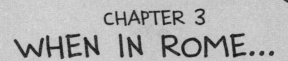

AS CAPTAIN FACT and Knowledge stepped into Ancient Rome, the Time Portal fizzled and faded behind them.

'We've made it!' said Captain Fact, as he looked around awestruck at the magnificent buildings that surrounded them. 'I feel overwhelmed, overcome and overexcited, all at the same time.'

'Well, I feel overcooked, overfizzled and thoroughly overegged,' said a shaky Knowledge. 'That Time Portal always leaves me mangled ...

Anyway, what is this place?' he asked. 'It looks like some sort of overcrowded market.'

'This isn't any old overcrowded market, Knowledge,' said Captain Fact. 'Ker-Fact! This is the Forum, the heart of Ancient Rome. It's full of the finest temples, the biggest bustling businesses and the most monumental monuments.' Captain Fact was rudely interrupted by a loud blasting on a horn and the ground began to shudder. 'Quick, hide behind a column,' he said.

Suddenly the Forum was filled by a huge file of soldiers, musicians, and prisoners. All around, people were cheering at the noisy procession.

'It's the longest queue I've ever seen,' said Knowledge. 'Is there a special offer on dog biscuits at the local supermarket?'

'Don't be ridiculous, Knowledge,' said Captain Fact. 'We've stumbled into a Triumphal Procession. Ker-Fact! Whenever the Roman Empire had a great triumph they held a victory parade. And we're right in the middle of one!' And with that Captain Fact's chin began to tremble . . .

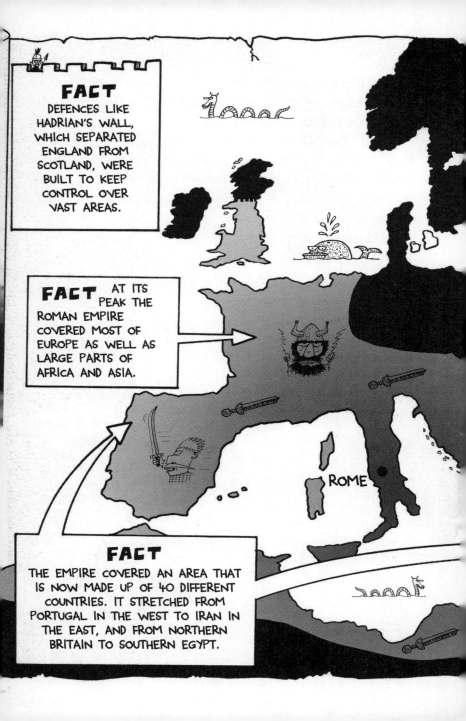

FACT
DEFENCES LIKE HADRIAN'S WALL, WHICH SEPARATED ENGLAND FROM SCOTLAND, WERE BUILT TO KEEP CONTROL OVER VAST AREAS.

FACT AT ITS PEAK THE ROMAN EMPIRE COVERED MOST OF EUROPE AS WELL AS LARGE PARTS OF AFRICA AND ASIA.

ROME

FACT
THE EMPIRE COVERED AN AREA THAT IS NOW MADE UP OF 40 DIFFERENT COUNTRIES. IT STRETCHED FROM PORTUGAL IN THE WEST TO IRAN IN THE EAST, AND FROM NORTHERN BRITAIN TO SOUTHERN EGYPT.

The procession seemed to carry on forever as the two superheroes looked on in wonderment.

'Great procession. But where are the snacks?' said Knowledge. 'They may have mountains of treasure but can they make popcorn? Where are the hot dog stands? I'm not seeing milkshakes.'

'There's no time for snacks, Knowledge,' said Captain Fact, scanning the horizon, 'we've got a museum to save. And look, there's the Colosseum. We need to slip past these guards and get across the procession. Follow me.'

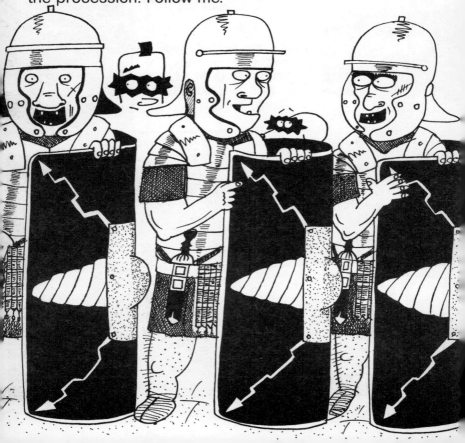

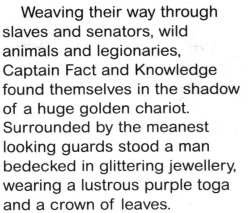

Weaving their way through slaves and senators, wild animals and legionaries, Captain Fact and Knowledge found themselves in the shadow of a huge golden chariot. Surrounded by the meanest looking guards stood a man bedecked in glittering jewellery, wearing a lustrous purple toga and a crown of leaves.

'Who's the pompous man wearing a salad?' asked Knowledge, looking up.

'That must be the Emperor,' said Captain Fact. 'Ker-Fact! The laurel wreath, a crown made out of laurel leaves, was used to symbolise victory.' With that his quiff began to quiver ...

'Seize them!' screeched the Emperor, as he became aware of the odd figures at the foot of his chariot. 'Who is this strangely dressed man and dog-creature that dare approach his Imperial Majesty?!?'

And with that Captain Fact and Knowledge were bundled up by a menacing Roman guard and dragged away ...

CHAPTER 4
HANNIBAL LECTURE

THE NEXT THING they knew Captain Fact and Knowledge were being carried through a huge gate into an enclosed courtyard.

'Why are we being taken into a camp site?' asked Knowledge as he looked around him. 'If I'd known we were going to a holiday camp I'd have brought my swimming trunks.'

'This isn't a holiday camp, Knowledge,' said Captain Fact nervously. 'This is the camp of the Praetorian Guard. Ker-Fact! The Praetorian Guard were the Emperor's personal bodyguards and the most feared soldiers in Rome.'

'Mmm,' pondered Knowledge, 'and I get the impression they've taken a dislike to us.'

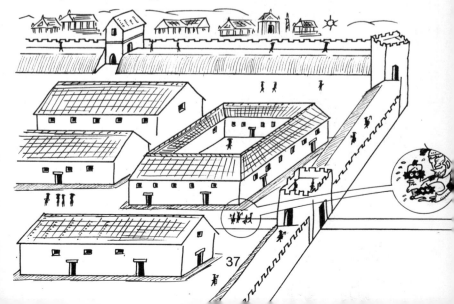

The guard holding Captain Fact and Knowledge strode through the courtyard to a small doorway. After a brief conversation with the jailer, our two superheroes were unceremoniously thrown into a dank dungeon.

As Captain Fact surveyed their bleak surroundings, Knowledge was making himself comfortable.

'There's no time to have a rest, Knowledge,' said Captain Fact. 'We've got to save the Tickell Museum and everyone inside it.'

'But we'll never get out of here,' said Knowledge, snuggling up in the straw. 'The place is swarming with soldiers.'

Sure enough, through the window, as far as the eye could see were Roman soldiers, marching, training, drilling.

'The Roman Army was one of the most awesome in history,' said Captain Fact as his cape flapped . . .

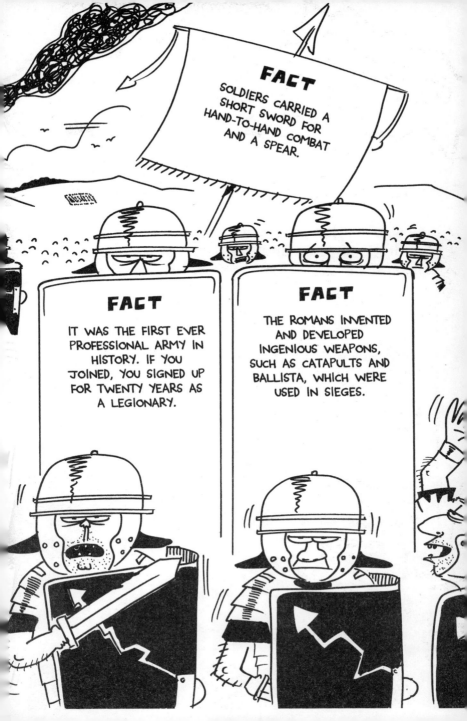

'Wake up, Knowledge, I've had an idea to get us out of here,' said Captain Fact urgently. 'Repeat with me: "Hannibal is at the gates".'

'Hanni-who?' asked Knowledge grumpily. 'I was dreaming that I was locked in a dog-biscuit warehouse.'

'Hannibal, he was the most feared enemy of Ancient Rome,' said Captain Fact breathlessly. 'And the saying "Hannibal is at the gates" was used for hundreds of years after his defeat to scare children. Let's see if it works on the jailer.'

'I suppose we could try,' said Knowledge wiping the sleep from his eyes. Standing behind the door the two started chanting:

The dungeon door creaked open and a nervous jailer stepped in.

'NOW, KNOWLEDGE, RUN! I'LL GRAB HIS SWORD!' shouted Captain Fact, and the two of them dashed through the door and slammed it behind them.

'Free! We're free!' cried Knowledge triumphantly but Captain Fact was already aware that the entire camp was staring at them.

'Um, not just yet, Knowledge,' gulped Captain Fact. All around them the Praetorian Guard were drawing their swords and closing in.

'Over there, Knowledge,' said Captain Fact, pointing at a wooden contraption. 'It's our only hope.'

'Climbing frame! Brilliant!' said Knowledge delightedly.

'That's no climbing frame,' said Captain Fact as they jumped into the rock-holder, 'it's a catapult.' And with that Captain Fact cut the rope and released the catapult ...

CHAPTER 5
ROME ALONE

CAPTAIN FACT AND Knowledge sailed out of the camp, over the Colosseum and through the Roman sky . . . and it soon became clear they were heading straight for an imposing building.

'We're doomed!' cried Knowledge, 'I never thought I'd end my days splattered on a Roman roof.'

'Not so fast, Knowledge,' shouted Captain Fact. 'By my calculations we should pass safely through the traditional Roman sky liiiiiiight . . .'

S P L O O S H !

Captain Fact and Knowledge landed with a splash.

'We made it!' spluttered Knowledge. 'Saved by a Roman aquarium!'

'This isn't an aquarium, Knowledge,' said Captain Fact. 'Ker-Fact! This is an *impluvium*, an ornamental pool that was the centre-piece of wealthy Roman houses.'

Captain Fact shook himself down. 'Let's get out of here Knowledge. Follow me.'

But Knowledge was already heading into a side room.

'Come back at once,' said Captain Fact sternly. 'Where do you think you're going?'

'But I can smell the finest cuisine my nose has ever encountered,' replied Knowledge excitedly.

'An archaeologist and a class of children are depending on us,' said Captain Fact as he sniffed the air. 'That dish is Mouse Cooked in Honey and Poppy Seeds, an Ancient Roman speciality. Through there must be the kitchen ...' And with that his nose began to twitch ...

PROPERTIES

!!
BRITANNIA
Villa with great 'Edge of Empire' location
FACT
ANCIENT ROMANS DIDN'T EAT MUCH DURING THE DAY, SO THE KITCHEN ONLY REALLY SPRANG INTO LIFE FOR THE EVENING MEAL. BUT THAT STARTED AT TWO OR THREE IN THE AFTERNOON AND WENT ON FOR SEVERAL HOURS!
POMPEII
Fabulous views of Vesuvius
FACT
ONLY THE WEALTHIEST COULD AFFORD GLASS WINDOWS, THE REST COVERED THEIRS WITH ANIMAL HIDES.
GAUL
Close to vineyards

'What's wrong?' asked Captain Fact anxiously.

'I'm smelling dog,' said Knowledge, freezing, 'and not of the friendly variety.'

'Ker-Fact! The Romans used to keep ferocious guard dogs,' said Captain Fact as the growling turned into a spine-tingling bark. 'Can't you talk to him?'

'I don't speak doggie Latin,' said Knowledge nervously.

WOOF!
WOOF!

The dog's barking had brought the house to life, and people were emerging from every doorway to see what was going on.

'Who are all these people?' asked Knowledge.

'They are slaves,' said Captain Fact, and with that his elbow began to itch . . .

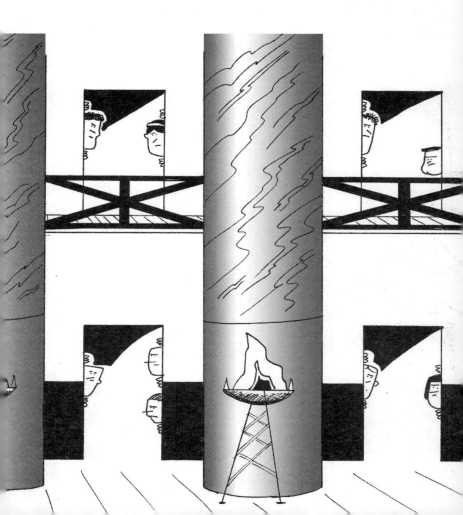

With the front entrance blocked, Captain Fact had to find another way out quickly. 'Time to use the Power of Fact,' said Captain Fact decisively. 'Roman houses had an enclosed rear garden, which had an exit onto the back street . . . it's our only way out.'

CHAPTER 6
BATH TIME!

BACK ON THE street, Captain Fact and Knowledge locked on to the Colosseum and headed towards it as fast as their legs would carry them. Weaving their way through the back streets, past grocers, bakeries and butchers, Captain Fact and Knowledge were finally making good progress.

'We should be there in no time,' said Captain Fact gleefully.

But Captain Fact had spoken too soon, and as they turned a corner they were once again confronted by a group of Praetorian Guards.

'I'm not getting in that catapult again,' wailed Knowledge.

'I've got an idea,' said Captain Fact, as the guards spotted them. 'Follow me.'

Captain Fact and Knowledge dashed through an impressive doorway, with the guards in hot pursuit.

'It's a Roman baths!' said Captain Fact. 'Let's hide in here!' He looked around for a hiding place.

'This way,' he said as he entered a hot and steamy room. 'Ker-Fact! This is the *suditorium,* the sauna. They'll never spot us in here.'

And with that his brow began to sweat . . .

FACT

FACT
ONLY THE VERY RICH HAD BATHS IN THEIR OWN HOME, SO MOST PEOPLE MADE A DAILY TRIP TO THE PUBLIC BATH HOUSE.

FACT
THERE WAS NO SOAP. INSTEAD ROMANS WOULD SMEAR THEIR BODIES IN OIL, THEN SCRAPE OFF THE DIRT WITH A SCRAPER CALLED A STRIGIL

FACT
BEFORE BATHING ROMANS BUILT UP A SWEAT BY EXERCISING. MEN WOULD WRESTLE, FENCE AND LIFT WEIGHTS. WOMEN WOULD ROLL A HOOP.

When they were sure that the Praetorian Guards had moved on, Captain Fact and Knowledge emerged from the *suditorium*.

'I don't feel right,' said Captain Fact, suddenly feeling a bit tight under the armpits.

'I'm not surprised,' chuckled Knowledge, 'your outfit's shrunk.'

With a museum to save, Captain Fact and Knowledge grabbed the first set of clothes they came across.

'Red doesn't usually suit me, but they'll have to do,' said Captain Fact, looking down at his new found outfit. 'To the Colosseum!'

CHAPTER 7
NEED FOR SPEED

BACK ON THE street, the Praetorian Guards were long gone but in their place was a large crowd, all heading in the same direction. When they spotted Captain Fact and Knowledge, the throng froze as one.

'Why are they all staring at us?' whispered Knowledge urgently.

But before Captain Fact could reply they had been swept off their feet and were carried, shoulder high, through the streets of Rome.

Although Captain Fact and Knowledge were being swept off against their will, the cheering crowd seemed friendly. It wasn't long before they were at the gates of a vast stadium.

'Where are they taking us?' asked Knowledge.

'I do believe it's the Circus Maximus,' said Captain Fact.

'Circus?' inquired Knowledge. 'Does that mean clowns and trapeze artists?'

'Not that kind of circus,' replied Captain Fact. 'The Circus Maximus was Rome's greatest race track.'

'So why are they taking us here?' asked Knowledge.

'I know,' said Captain Fact, 'it's these clothes. We've accidentally put on charioteer outfits.'

'And that means . . . ?' continued Knowledge tremulously.

'That means they think we're in the next race!' said Captain Fact. No sooner had he said it than the two of them were bundled into a chariot at the start of the race.

Captain Fact's wrists began to wobble . . .

There was an ear-splitting blast from a trumpet and they were off! The crowd cheered as the horses bolted out of the starting gate.

'Hold on, Knowledge!' cried Captain Fact. 'We're in for a bumpy ride . . .'

As they came round the bend for the seventh time, Captain Fact and Knowledge were in the lead!

They passed the finishing post and the crowd
went wild!

'We've won! We've won!' squealed Knowledge.
'Where's the brake?'

'Brake, hmmm,' pondered Captain Fact. 'We
need to pull on the reins.'

But it was too late and the horses pounded on,
through the exit and back onto the street.

YIPPEEE!!!

CHAPTER 8
GAME ON

'HOW ARE WE going to get off?' wailed Knowledge, as their chariot sped through the streets of Rome.

'Get off?' said Captain Fact. 'You must be joking. This chariot is heading straight for the Colosseum!' Sure enough they were getting closer and closer to their goal.

'Let's hope the Museum can hold on a bit longer!' said Captain Fact as the Colosseum finally loomed up in front of them.

But instead of stopping at the gates, allowing Captain Fact and Knowledge to get off and find the gladiator school, the chariot hurtled on, into the Colosseum.

'We've made it! We've made it!' cried Knowledge, as they stepped down from the chariot. The horses then galloped off, leaving our superheroes stranded in the middle of the arena.

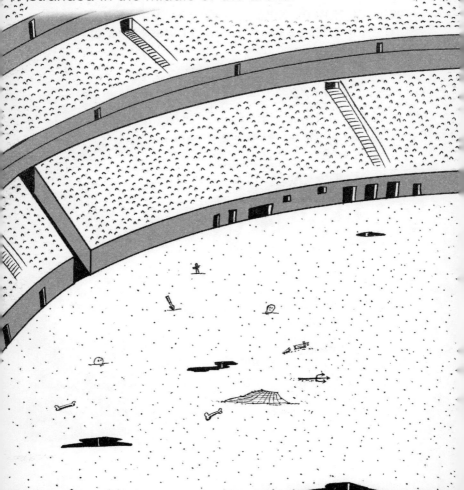

But delight soon turned to despair as the doors slammed shut behind them!

'So what *does* go on here?' asked Knowledge nervously.

And as the metal gates on the surrounding entrances started to creak open ominously, Captain Fact's nose began to itch . . .

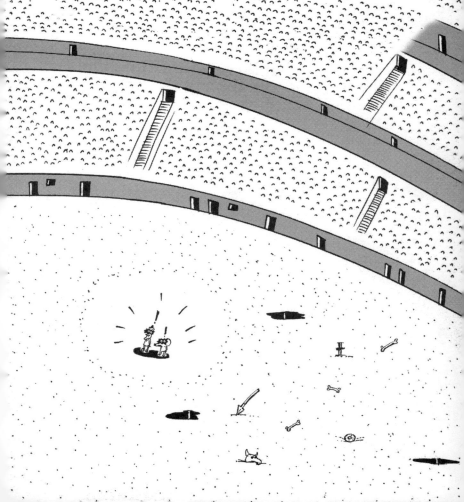

Souvenir Stall

FACT
THE GAMES WERE FREE BECAUSE THE EMPEROR PAID FOR THEM. THIS MADE HIM POPULAR WITH THE ROMAN PEOPLE.

FACT
TODAY, THE COLOSSEUM IS ONLY HALF THE BUILDING IT USED TO BE, BECAUSE LARGE PARTS OF IT HAVE BEEN REMOVED TO MAKE OTHER BUILDINGS. THIS ONLY STOPPED HAPPENING IN THE MIDDLE AGES.

FACT
SAND WAS PLACED ON THE GROUND TO SOAK UP THE BLOOD.

FACT
THE FLOOR WAS SOMETIMES FLOODED AND SHIPS BROUGHT IN SO GLADIATORS COULD RE-ENACT GREAT SEA BATTLES.

ATTACK!!!

Gladiators of every shape and size were closing in on Captain Fact and Knowledge.

'They think we're part of the show,' whispered Captain Fact.

'So, do we have a race, like at the Circus Maximus?' asked Knowledge hopefully.

'No,' said Captain Fact bluntly. 'We have a fight . . . *gulp* . . . to the death.'

As the gladiators encircled our intrepid superheroes, Captain Fact evaluated their situation.

'You don't have any weapons on you, by any chance?' asked Captain Fact optimistically.

'Only a bag of cinnamon-flavoured dog biscuits,' said Knowledge, 'I could throw them in a gladiator's face.'

'I don't think that's going to work,' said Captain Fact grimly. 'Time to press the emergency button on the Fact Watch.'

75

The gladiators all froze as a blood-curdling roar shook the Colosseum to its foundations.

'It's Factorella!' shouted Captain Fact and Knowledge. Sat on the back of a huge tiger was Professor Miniscule's daughter.

'Hi guys! You in trouble again?' said Factorella as the tiger bounded over the terrified gladiators to where Captain Fact and Knowledge were standing.

'Great to see you, Factorella,' said Captain Fact gratefully. 'We were having a spot of bother.'

'Jump on board, the gladiator school is just outside!'

Captain Fact and Knowledge hopped on the back of the tiger, which quickly bounded out of the Colosseum and onto the street.

'There you go,' said Factorella, as she dropped off Captain Fact and Knowledge.

'Check out the Time Flap,' said Factorella. 'It's Dad's latest invention – the world's first time travel cat-flap. As soon as I've taken this tiger to the jungle it's back to the present to change the oil on the Fact Scooters.' And with that she was gone.

CHAPTER 9
BACK TO SCHOOL

'HERE WE ARE, Knowledge,' said Captain Fact as they cautiously approached the entrance to the gladiator school. 'We've got to get in and find what's going to cause it to collapse in 2,000 years' time. Trouble is the gates are firmly shut.'

'So this is where the gladiators learned to read and write?' asked Knowledge.

'No, Knowledge, it's not that kind of school. Gladiator schools were the places where gladiators trained to fight each other.' And with that Captain Fact's knuckles began to throb . . .

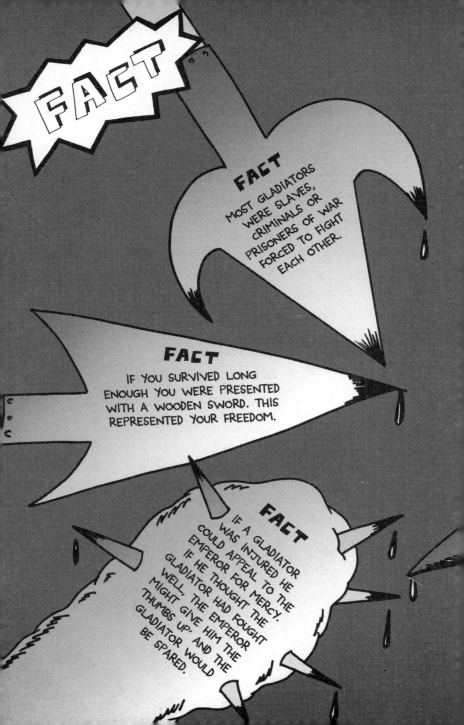

FACT

THERE WERE SEVERAL TYPES OF GLADIATOR.
EACH HAD A DIFFERENT WAY OF FIGHTING
AND DIFFERENT WEAPONS.

FACT

A THRACIAN GLADIATOR: USED A CURVED DAGGER
AND A SMALL ROUND SHIELD.
A RETIARIUS: HAD A NET TO TRAP HIS
OPPONENT AND A TRIDENT.
A MURMILLO: HAD A HEAVY SWORD AND
SHIELD AND A HELMET TOPPED WITH A FISH.

ATTACK!!!

Suddenly a huge cart trundled into view heading straight for the gates of the gladiator school.

'This is our chance, Knowledge!' whispered Captain Fact excitedly. 'Let's hop on the back of this. I calculate it should take us right into the heart of the gladiator school.' With a loud clanking noise Captain Fact and Knowledge found themselves on the back of the cart.

'I'd hoped it would be delivering lunch,' said Knowledge disappointedly.

But instead of a tasty Roman feast the cart was carrying equipment for the gladiator school. It was piled high with helmets, swords, spears and shields.

'I was hoping school would be out,' said Captain Fact nervously, 'but it looks like we're going to be in the thick of it.'

As the cart ground to a halt in the middle of the school, they were suddenly surrounded by gladiators grabbing weapons from the cart.

'Time to go undercover,' said Captain Fact.

'Again?' moaned Knowledge.

'We'll need to pretend to be gladiators if we're going to go unnoticed.' And with that Captain Fact whipped on a helmet and grabbed a trident.

Captain Fact and Knowledge did their best to blend in as a pair of sparring gladiators:

all around them men were shouting, grunting and groaning.

Swords clashed with shields and instructors barked out orders.

'They don't seem to have noticed us,' whispered Captain Fact as he prodded Knowledge's tummy with his trident.

'What did you do that for?' whined Knowledge. 'That hurt.'

'For goodness sake, Knowledge, we're trying to appear to be some of the most feared warriors of Ancient Rome,' said Captain Fact.

'OK,' said Knowledge, 'take that!' And he proceeded to batter Captain Fact on the shins with his sword.

'That's enough!' winced Captain Fact. 'We need to check out the basement.'

Leaving the gladiators behind them our intrepid superheroes heaved open the trapdoor and looked down into a dank, sweltering, stinking basement.

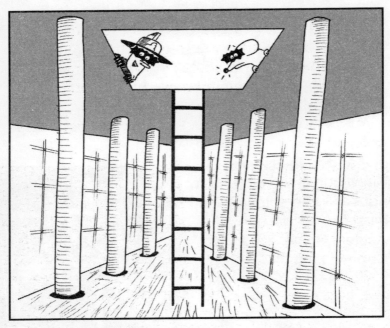

'The whole building is held up by these columns,' said Captain Fact as he descended the ladder.

'Never mind the columns, what's that terrible smell?' asked Knowledge, sniffing the air.

'Wild animals!' said Captain Fact. 'Ker-Fact! Gladiators would battle wild animals from all over the Roman Empire. This must be where they're kept.'

CHAPTER 10
CHAIN PAIN

AS CAPTAIN FACT'S and Knowledge's eyes
adjusted to the dark, they saw that they were
surrounded by cages containing wild animals.

'They've got everything down here,' said
Knowledge, 'lions, tigers . . .'

'And elephants!' interrupted Captain Fact. 'We've
cracked it!'

Chained to the central pillar was a colossal African elephant.

'Look at the way it's tugging on its chain,' said Captain Fact. 'That's what weakened the building. We have to free the elephant before it causes enough damage to have twenty-first-century ramifications.'

Captain Fact and Knowledge
began to hack at the chain
tethering the elephant to the pillar.
In no time they'd freed the animal.

'We've done it!' cried Captain Fact as he
examined the pillar. 'Just in time. This should
now be sturdy enough to ensure the Tickell
Museum does not collapse. Knowledge, free these
animals. I'll contact Professor Miniscule.'

'*Buzz – crackle* – congratulations, Captain Fact! Thanks to you the Museum has been saved and all those inside it got out in one piece – *crackle*. I should have guessed the supporting pillars may have been the weak spot, but I'd never have – *buzz* – guessed that an elephant was causing it.'

YOU'VE DONE IT, FACT!

'I see you've sent the Time Flap,' said Captain Fact as he heard a crackle behind him.

'Yes.' said Professor Miniscule. 'It's to set the animals free.'

Knowledge opened all the cages and ushered the wild animals through the Time Flap to freedom.

'That's the last animal gone,' said Knowledge. 'Can we go home now?'

'One last job,' crackled Professor Miniscule. 'I want you to put that basement out of action forever!'

'I've got an idea,' said Captain Fact. 'I do believe that's a bag of lime. Give that pipe a thump, Knowledge. The water will react with the lime and this volcanic soil to make concrete. That will seal this place up for good.'

As the water began to rise around them, and the mixture started to bubble up and harden, the Time Portal began to materialise.

CHAPTER 11
AND NOW THE WEATHER . . .

ONCE AGAIN THE Time Portal's co-ordinates were a bit wonky. Instead of stepping out into their office they stepped straight into the canteen.

It was Italian Food Day and the Boss was tucking into pizza, spaghetti, ravioli and ice cream, when suddenly Captain Fact and Knowledge, still in their gladiator outfits, materialised in his bowl of food.

'Cliff, Puddles? What's going on?' mumbled the Boss. 'I know it's Italian Food Day, but why are you wearing those outfits, and what are you doing in my spaghetti?!'

But before you could say 'tiramisu', Cliff and Puddles were back in their office and changing out of their outfits, ready for their evening weather forecast.

Lucy in the Make-up Department couldn't wait to tell them the news.

'Captain Fact has done it again!' gushed Lucy. 'He's so brave! He went back to Ancient Rome and saved the building, Sir Ramsbottom and the kids. I'd like to have Captain Fact as an exhibit in *my* museum!'

Cliff blushed as he strode through the door, on to the studio floor and stepped in front of the cameras.

And so, with the Tickell Museum saved and Sir Ramsbottom and the school kids safely home, Cliff Thornhill and Puddles were back doing what they did worst – the weather!

Until the next crisis . . .

CAPTAIN FACT'S SPACE ADVENTURE

CAPTAIN FACT'S DINOSAUR ADVENTURE

CAPTAIN FACT'S CREEPY-CRAWLY

ADVENTURE

CAPTAIN FACT'S EGYPTIAN ADVENTURE

AND

CAPTAIN FACT'S HUMAN

BODY ADVENTURE

ARE AVAILABLE IN
BOOKSHOPS NOW!